This Book

belongs to
Brashilla
Santos

Biannery

Altagracia

Lizardo

Mejia

Vargas.

THE
Red Shoes

In memory of my daughter, Maura—
the beautiful bird who flew away

Many thanks to my ever–helpful and supportive husband Stan;
Judy, Andrea, and Hilary; Riff; the children at Braly School
(especially Steven) in Sunnyvale, California; and, of course, Lou
and Kim for their advice and confidence in me.

Paperback edition published in 2000
Text and illustrations copyright © 1997 by Barbara Bazilian

A **Whispering Coyote** Book
Published by Charlesbridge Publishing
85 Main Street
Watertown, MA 02472
(617) 926-0329
www.charlesbridge.com

Library of Congress Cataloging–in–Publication Data

Bazilian, Barbara, 1933–
The red shoes / written and illustrated by Barbara Bazilian.
p. cm.
Summary: A retelling of the Hans Christian Andersen fairy tale in which a girl's desire for
a pair of red dancing shoes almost dooms her to dance forever.
ISBN 1–879085–56–9 (reinforced for library use)
ISBN 1-58089-069-5 (softcover)
[1. Fairy tales. 2. Shoes—Fiction. 3. Pride and vanity—Fiction.]
I. Andersen, H.C. (Hans Christian), 1804–1875. Røde sko. II. Title.
PZ7.B34755Re 1997
[E]—dc20   96–29257

(HC) 10 9 8 7 6 5 4 3 2
(SC) 10 9 8 7 6 5 4 3 2 1

Book design and production by *The Kids at Our House*
Text set in 14-point Caslon 224 Book
Printed in Hong Kong

THE
Red Shoes

✦ ✦ ✦

ADAPTED FROM A STORY BY
HANS CHRISTIAN ANDERSEN

RETOLD AND ILLUSTRATED BY
BARBARA BAZILIAN

🐾 Whispering Coyote
A Charlesbridge Imprint

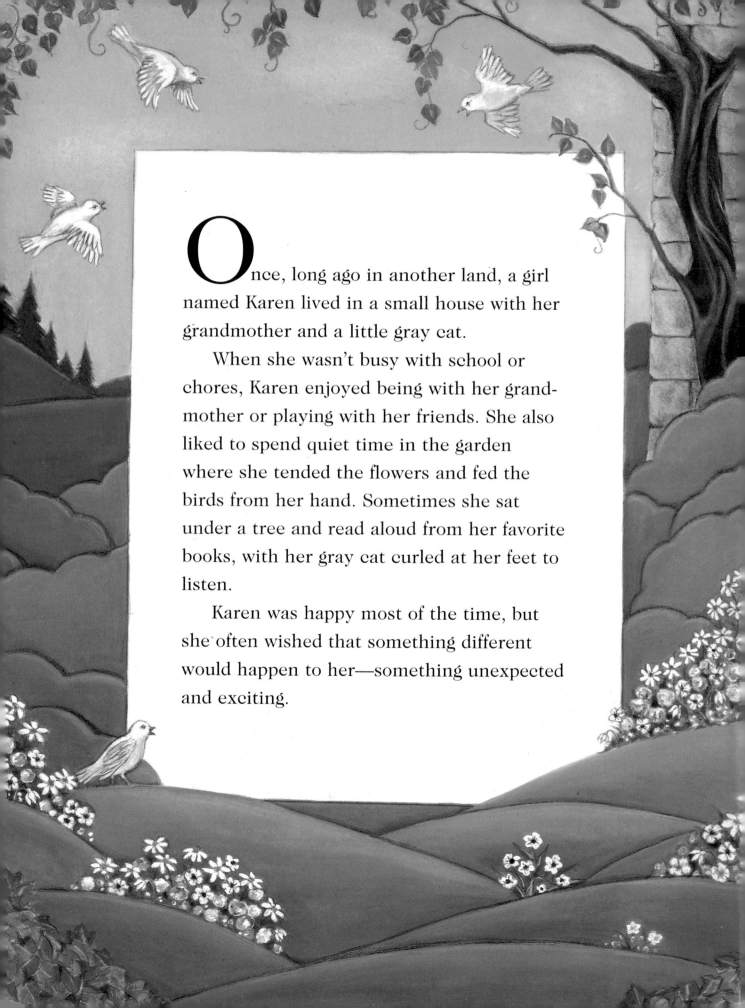

Once, long ago in another land, a girl named Karen lived in a small house with her grandmother and a little gray cat.

When she wasn't busy with school or chores, Karen enjoyed being with her grandmother or playing with her friends. She also liked to spend quiet time in the garden where she tended the flowers and fed the birds from her hand. Sometimes she sat under a tree and read aloud from her favorite books, with her gray cat curled at her feet to listen.

Karen was happy most of the time, but she often wished that something different would happen to her—something unexpected and exciting.

One day, Karen's grandmother took her to the shoemaker's shop for new shoes. Karen looked into the shop window, and there she saw a pair of beautiful red dancing shoes with long silk ribbons. She wanted those shoes more than anything else in the world.

Karen tugged at her grandmother's sleeve. "Grandmama," she said eagerly, "can we buy the red shoes?"

"No," said her grandmother. "They're too bright for school, and they'll wear out quickly. We'll buy you a nice pair of black shoes with silver buckles." At any other time, Karen would have liked her new shoes, but after seeing the red shoes they seemed ugly to her.

After Karen's grandmother paid for the new shoes, she hurried Karen from the shop. Karen looked back longingly at the red shoes, which seemed to beckon to her from the shop window.

Even though her grandmother wouldn't buy her the red shoes, Karen couldn't stop thinking about them. Whenever she could, she went past the shoemaker's shop to look at them in the window and wish they were hers.

Karen said nothing to her grandmother about wanting the red shoes, but every week she secretly put a few coins from her spending money into a glass jar. She dreamed about the day when she would have enough money to buy the red dancing shoes.

Time went by. Karen began to spend almost all her time daydreaming about the red shoes. She thought about them the last thing at night, the first thing in the morning, and all through the day.

Sometimes, instead of doing her homework, Karen whirled and curtsied in front of her mirror. She imagined that she was wearing the red shoes and that all her friends were jealous of how beautiful she looked.

Her daydreams became more important than the things she once liked doing. She stopped playing with her friends and forgot to tend the flowers and feed the birds. When her grandmother asked her to do something, Karen slammed her bedroom door and said, "Leave me alone! I'll do it later!"

A few years later, a new city hall was built. There was to be a grand ball to celebrate the occasion, and everyone in the town was invited. Karen had never stopped wishing for the red shoes, and she felt she must have them to wear to the ball. She took out her glass jar and counted the coins. At last she had enough money to buy the shoes!

Without telling her grandmother, Karen ran to the old shoemaker's shop and gave him the jar of coins. "I want to buy the red dancing shoes," she said. "I've wished for nothing else ever since I first saw them." As the old shoemaker wrapped the shoes, he smiled in a mysterious way. "Be careful what you wish for," he said softly, "because it may come true." Karen felt a little frightened when he said this, but she soon forget everything else in her excitement.

That night after supper, Karen put on the red shoes and tied the long silk ribbons. "At last they're mine!" she thought. "Everyone will be jealous of me!" She slipped quietly out of the house and ran down the path into the forest. She whirled and danced among the trees. Wearing the shoes made her feel as light and graceful as the wind—as if her feet were not even touching the ground.

She had an odd sense of being swept along until she could hardly breathe. It was a scary feeling, but exciting at the same time. As she danced, Karen thought, "No one has ever danced this well. I don't ever want to stop." When Karen returned to her room, she didn't want to take the shoes off. As if the shoes knew what she was feeling, they seemed to stick to her feet a little as she untied the ribbons.

Karen knew that her grandmother would scold her for buying the red shoes without permission, so she hid them in her closet. Every night she took them out and admired them in secret.

On the night of the ball, Karen put on her best dress. She slipped her feet into the red shoes and tied the ribbons carefully. Then she stood in front of her mirror and admired herself. "The red shoes make me look beautiful," she thought, "and they'll make me dance better than anyone else at the ball."

Karen's grandmother had decided not to go to the ball and was napping in her room. Karen didn't want her grandmother to see her wearing the red shoes, so she tip-toed past her grandmother's room and slipped quietly out of the house without waking her.

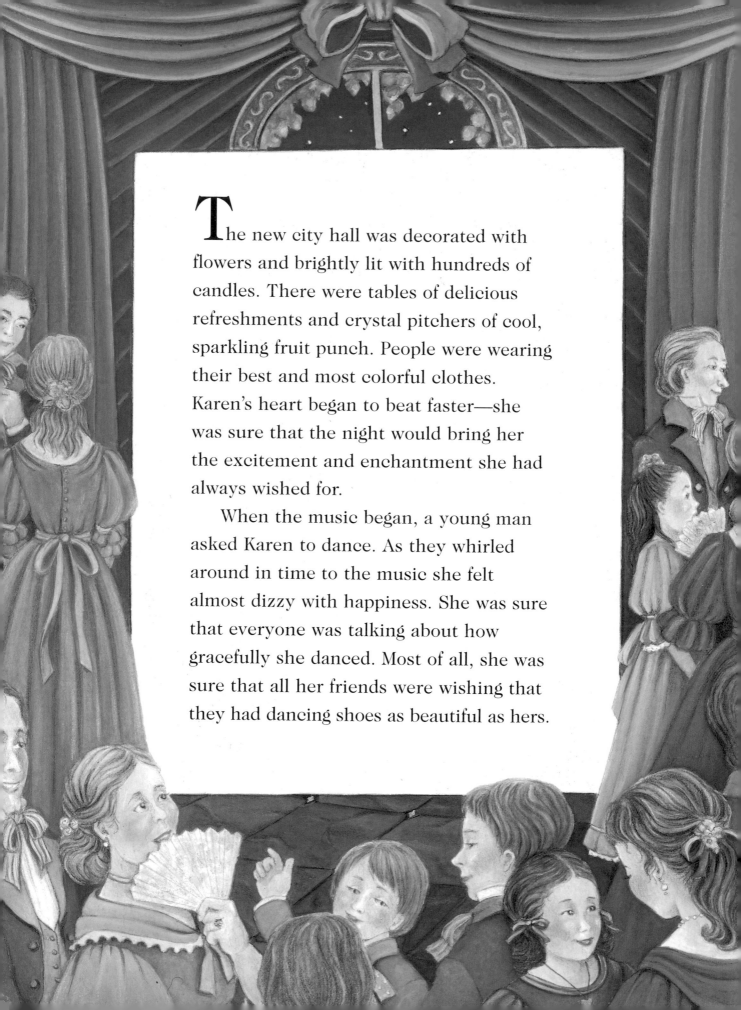

The new city hall was decorated with flowers and brightly lit with hundreds of candles. There were tables of delicious refreshments and crystal pitchers of cool, sparkling fruit punch. People were wearing their best and most colorful clothes. Karen's heart began to beat faster—she was sure that the night would bring her the excitement and enchantment she had always wished for.

When the music began, a young man asked Karen to dance. As they whirled around in time to the music she felt almost dizzy with happiness. She was sure that everyone was talking about how gracefully she danced. Most of all, she was sure that all her friends were wishing that they had dancing shoes as beautiful as hers.

After Karen had been dancing for what seemed like hours, she suddenly found herself near the old shoemaker. He pointed to her feet and said, "What beautiful dancing shoes! They will stick fast when you dance!" For a moment Karen felt uneasy, but the excitement of the dancing soon made her forget his words.

Then Karen noticed that she was not always dancing in the direction she wanted to go. The red shoes seemed to have a mind of their own. It was as if they would not let her do what she wanted to do.

Soon she began to feel like a puppet on strings. When she wanted to go to the right, the shoes seemed to pull her to the left. When she wanted to go to one end of the room, the shoes seemed to dance her to the other end. "This feels very strange," Karen thought.

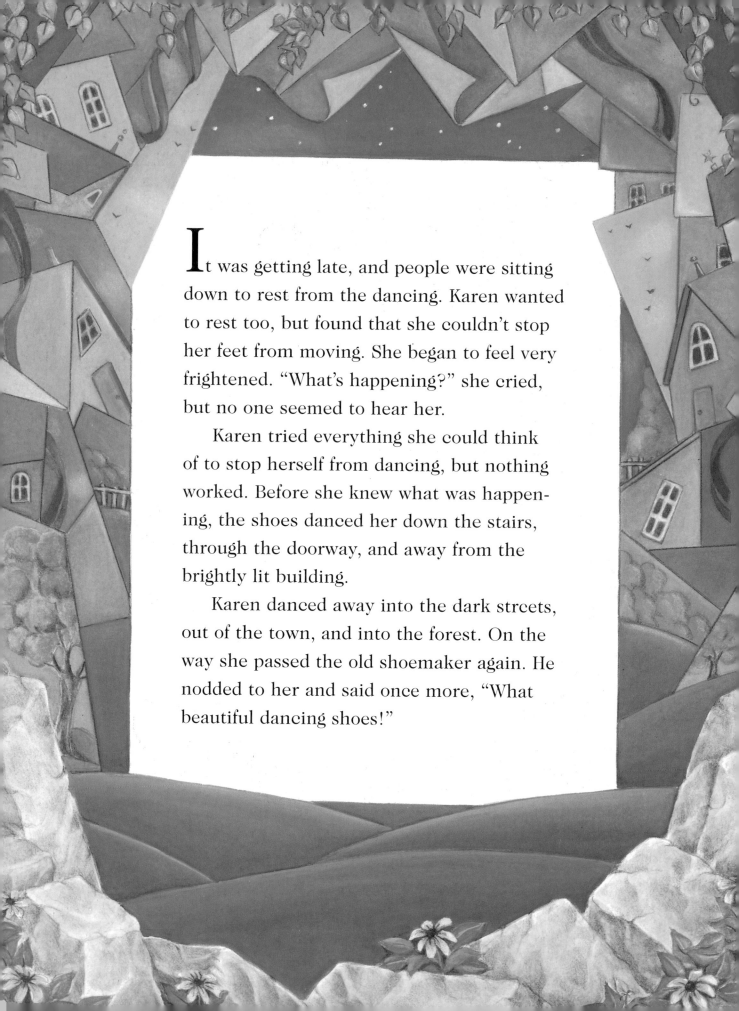

It was getting late, and people were sitting down to rest from the dancing. Karen wanted to rest too, but found that she couldn't stop her feet from moving. She began to feel very frightened. "What's happening?" she cried, but no one seemed to hear her.

Karen tried everything she could think of to stop herself from dancing, but nothing worked. Before she knew what was happening, the shoes danced her down the stairs, through the doorway, and away from the brightly lit building.

Karen danced away into the dark streets, out of the town, and into the forest. On the way she passed the old shoemaker again. He nodded to her and said once more, "What beautiful dancing shoes!"

Karen could not understand what was happening and felt more and more frightened. "The red shoes are making me dance," she thought. "I must take them off!"

She tried to untie the ribbons and she tugged at the shoes, but it was no use—the shoes were stuck to her feet. She kept pulling and tugging at them, but no matter what she did, the shoes would not come off.

She danced on and on. She felt very tired and tried to sit down on a tree stump, but the shoes would not let her rest. When she tried to stop dancing, her feet would not stay still. They kept kicking and moving until she had no choice but to get up and dance on.

Karen danced up and down the hills, through the woods, over roads and paths, fields and meadows, by day and by night, through rain and snow. She ate berries and drank rain water. Her clothes became dirty and torn, and her hair grew tangled and wild.

She was frightened and lonely, and had no idea where the shoes were taking her. She missed her grandmother and longed to be safe at home again.

On and on she went. Her feet were sore and bleeding, but the shoes wouldn't let her stop to rest. She passed many people and begged them to help her. They felt sorry for her and tried to pull the red shoes off her feet, but no one could do it.

Karen felt as if she had been dancing forever. Finally one night she saw the old shoemaker again. As she danced by, she called out to him, "I should never have wished so hard for the red shoes. Please help me take them off and end this spell so I can go home!"

"No," he answered. "You wished to dance in the red shoes, and dance you shall! You must keep dancing wherever the shoes may take you."

Karen begged him again to free her from the spell, but her shoes led her away before she heard his answer. The old shoemaker disappeared in the darkness behind her, and Karen was left alone to continue her endless dance.

One night, the red shoes danced Karen toward the edge of a steep cliff. Karen became very frightened and cried, "I wish I had wings to carry me through the air!" Suddenly, soft feathers began to grow from Karen's arms and body. The red shoes danced her over the edge of the cliff, but she didn't fall. She felt light and free. She had changed into a beautiful bird!

The night wind lifted her on her new wings. As she swooped and glided in the moonlight, the red shoes fell away from her—down, down toward the ground far below.

For many days Karen soared over the forest until she saw her grandmother's house. Her grandmother was sitting in the garden with the gray cat in her lap, looking very sad.

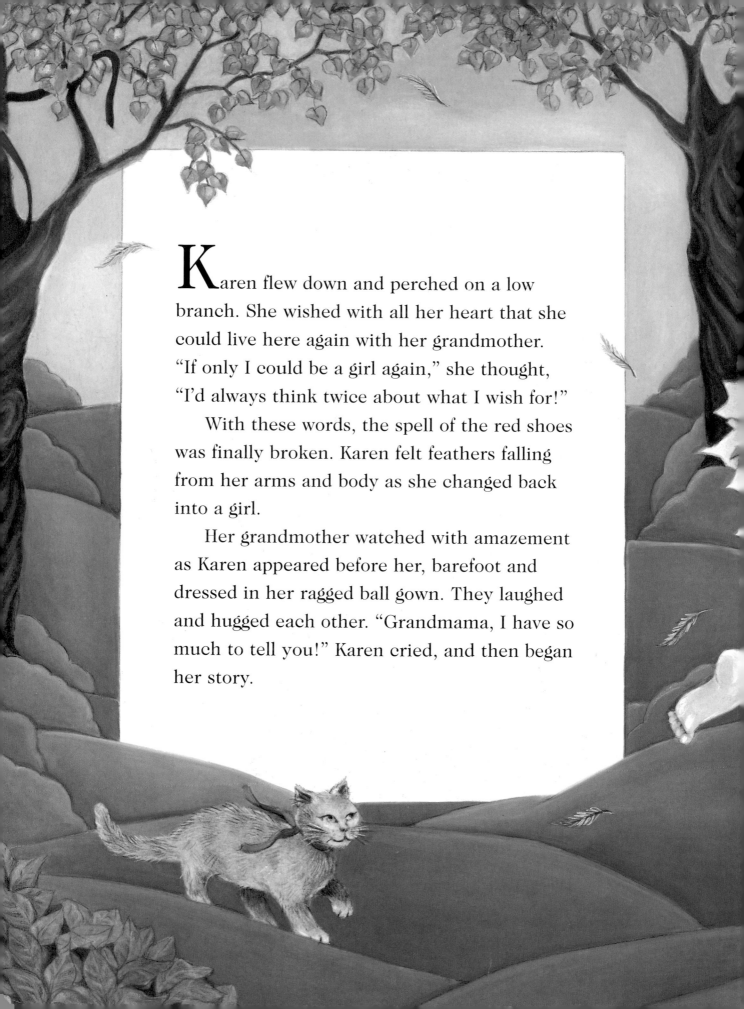

Karen flew down and perched on a low branch. She wished with all her heart that she could live here again with her grandmother. "If only I could be a girl again," she thought, "I'd always think twice about what I wish for!"

With these words, the spell of the red shoes was finally broken. Karen felt feathers falling from her arms and body as she changed back into a girl.

Her grandmother watched with amazement as Karen appeared before her, barefoot and dressed in her ragged ball gown. They laughed and hugged each other. "Grandmama, I have so much to tell you!" Karen cried, and then began her story.

Meanwhile, deep in the forest, the old shoemaker crept out from behind some bramble bushes. He picked up the red shoes where they had landed in a small clearing and carefully brushed off the bits of leaves and twigs that clung to them. Clutching the shoes tightly, he disappeared among the trees, never to be seen again.